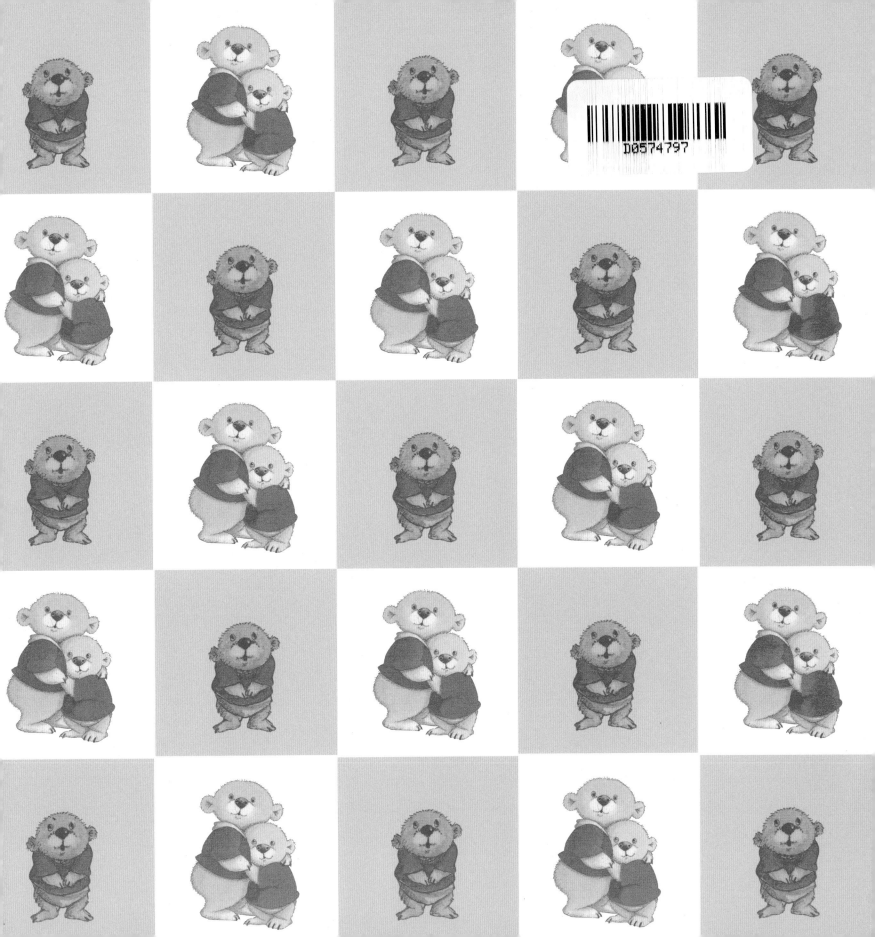

This book belongs to

HANUCHOE

HNHANUCHOE

For Jack Kitchin
and his Mum and Dad

N. McM.

First published in 2001 in Great Britain by
David & Charles Children's Books

© 2001 by Nigel McMullen

This 2010 edition published by Sandy Creek,
by arrangement with Gullane Children's Books.

Sandy Creek
122 Fifth Avenue
New York, NY 10011

ISBN: 978-1-4351-2273-4

Printed and bound in China

1 3 5 7 9 10 8 6 4 2

Not Me!

by Nigel McMullen

Jack thinks Kenny is the best brother in the world. At breakfast, when Jack knocked his plate on the floor and Mom came in looking angry…

Jack said, "It was him!"

Kenny, who was too young
to talk, said nothing.

At lunchtime, when Mom asked who had eaten the cake she'd taken all morning to make...

Jack said, "Not me!" and hid
the last slice in Kenny's diaper.

Kenny, who was too young
to care, sat down.

Jack was building mudpies when Mom called, "You'd better stay clean!"

Jack said, "I will," and cleaned his hands on Kenny's shirt.

Kenny, who was too young to know what mud was, thought it tasted great.

At bathtime, Jack was playing with the squirty soap when Mom asked who'd made all that mess...

Jack said, "It was him!" and handed the bottle to Kenny.

Kenny, who was too
young to know better,
squirted Mom.

Splish!

Splash!

When they were warm and sleepy and ready for bed, Mom looked at Kenny and sighed, "You're so much trouble! But we wouldn't swap him, would we, Jack?" Jack said, "Not me," and gave Kenny a kiss.

Kenny, who had never said anything before, chose that moment to say his very first word…